ANY KIND OF DOG

by Lynn Reiser

A Mulberry Paperback Book, New York

Watercolors and a black pen were
used for the full-color art.
The text type is Helvetica Light.

Copyright © 1992 by
Lynn Whisnant Reiser

Printed in the United States of America.
First Mulberry Edition, 1994

10 9 8 7 6 5 4

The Library of Congress has cataloged
the Greenwillow edition as follows:
Reiser, Lynn.
Any kind of dog/Lynn Reiser
    p. cm.
Summary:
All Richard wants is a dog,
even though his mother
tries to give him other
kinds of pets.
Mulberry ISBN 0-688-13572-2
[1 Pets—Fiction.
2. Dogs—Fiction.]
I. Title.
PZ7. R27745An 1992
[E]—dc20
91-12771 CIP AC

for Dick, Chris, and Mort,
who love dogs

Richard wanted a dog, any kind of dog.

But his mother said
a dog was
too much trouble,

so she gave him a caterpillar.

The caterpillar was very nice.
It looked a little like a dog,

Lhasa Apso

but it was not a dog.
Richard wanted a dog.
His mother said
a dog was too much trouble,

so she gave him a mouse.

The mouse was very nice.
It looked a little like a dog,

Chihuahua

but it was not a dog.
Richard wanted a dog.
His mother said
a dog was too much trouble,

so she gave him a baby alligator.

The baby alligator was very nice.
It looked a little like a dog,

Dachshund

but it was not a dog.
Richard wanted a dog.
His mother said
a dog was too much trouble,

so she gave him a lamb.

The lamb was very nice.
It looked a little like a dog,

Bedlington
Terrier

but it was not a dog.
Richard wanted a dog.
His mother said
a dog was too much trouble,

so she gave him a pony.

The pony was very nice.
It looked a little like a dog,

Great Dane

but it was not a dog.
Richard wanted a dog.
His mother said
a dog was too much trouble,

so she gave him a lion.

The lion was very nice.
It looked a little like a dog,

Chow Chow

but it was not a dog.
Richard wanted a dog.
His mother said
a dog was too much trouble,

so she gave him a bear.

The bear was very nice.
It looked a little like a dog,

Newfoundland

but it was not a dog.

All of the animals were very nice,

but Richard still wanted a dog.

So his mother gave him a dog.

The dog was very nice.
It looked exactly like a dog.

Just a Dog

The dog was a lot of trouble,

but
it was
worth it.